For Mum and Dad—Adam

A tale of consequences
by Adam Stower, called...

huff, puff, huf

Sizzle

First published in the United Kingdom by Templar Publishing

Copyright © 2005 by Adam Stower

Original edition published in English under the title of: SLAM!

Published in North America in 2014 by Owlkids Books Inc.

Owlkids Books acknowledges the financial support of the Canada Council for the Arts, the Ontario Arts Council, the Government of Canada through the Canada Book Fund (CBF) and the Government of Ontario through the Ontario Media Development Corporation's Book Initiative for our publishing activities.

Published in Canada by	Published in the United States by
Owlkids Books Inc.	Owlkids Books Inc.
10 Lower Spadina Avenue	1700 Fourth Street
Toronto, ON M5V 2Z2	Berkeley, CA 94710

Library and Archives Canada Cataloguing in Publication

Stower, Adam, author, illustrator
    Slam! : a tale of consequences / Adam Stower.

ISBN 978-1-77147-007-0 (bound)

    I. Title.

PZ7.S887Sl 2014   j823'.914   C2013-903741-1

Library of Congress Control Number: 2013942848

Manufactured in Dongguan, China, in September 2013, by Toppan Leefung Packaging & Printing (Dongguan) Co., Ltd.
Job #BAYDC5

A   B   C   D   E   F

 Publisher of Chirp, chickaDEE and OWL
www.owlkidsbooks.com